UNCLE TEASE

(5)

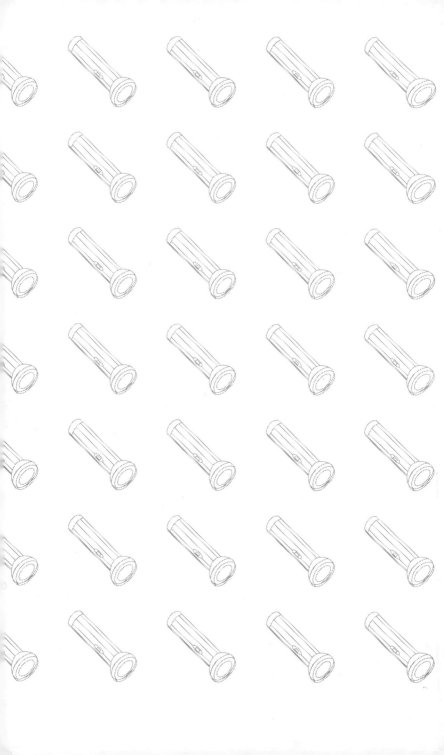

Contents

The Practical Joke 5

The Big News 10

Coded Messages 15

The Presentation 21

The List 27

The Party 32

The Postcard 39

Dits and Dahs 43

The True Story 47

The Flash Flood 54

The International
  Morse Code 61

The Practical Joke

Dorrie and D.J. searched the crowd of people coming off the plane.

"I can't see him," D.J. whispered to his twin sister.

"He'll be here," Dad said.

Dorrie looked down the tunnel that connected the plane to the terminal. The only person coming through the tunnel was a man holding a baby.

Uncle Tease didn't have a baby. He wasn't even married.

"I hope Uncle Tease never gets married," Dorrie said, thinking aloud.

"Me, too," D.J. said. "Married people aren't much fun."

"I bet that's him," Dorrie pointed. The approaching passenger did look like Uncle Tease. But he was carrying a briefcase and looked very businesslike.

Uncle Tease had never owned a briefcase in his life. He was always doing exciting things like floating in a balloon or rafting down the Amazon.

The next passenger was a tall man with glasses and a bushy moustache. He wore a huge cowboy hat.

The man looked around the room. Then he sat down on a bench. No one else appeared in the tunnel.

"Where can he be?" D.J. asked.

Dorrie was worried. "Maybe he missed his plane."

"Or Mum gave us the wrong flight number," Dad said. "I'd better phone her at home."

Just then, the man with the cowboy hat got up from the bench. "Hi," he said. "Perhaps you can help me. My niece and nephew were supposed to meet me here. They're twins. But they haven't recognized me yet..."

As he spoke, the man came closer, and Dorrie and D.J. noticed that the moustache looked false.

"Uncle Tease!" D.J. shouted and hugged his uncle. Uncle Tease planted the cowboy hat on D.J.'s head.

Dorrie hugged her uncle, too, as he stuck the moustache under her nose.

Dad was laughing. "Ted, you're terrible. No wonder the kids call you Uncle Tease."

Uncle Tease laughed, too. He took Dorrie and D.J.'s hands. "Come on," he said, "we have to go to the baggage-claim area. Have I got a surprise for you!"

The Big News

Dad unlocked the boot. He put a big box and Uncle Tease's duffle bag inside. The door barely closed.

"So, Ted, what's new?" Dad asked, once they were out on the road.

"Oh, you know, the usual – work, travel, marriage."

"What?" Dad shouted.

"Yes. We're making wedding plans." Uncle Tease winked at Dorrie and D.J.

Uncle Tease had wedding plans? Dorrie couldn't believe what her uncle was saying.

She looked at D.J. "He's teasing, isn't he?" she whispered.

"Well," D.J. answered, "why don't you ask him?"

"No way," Dorrie said. "If he's teasing about that, I don't want to encourage him. We should just change the subject."

She prodded Uncle Tease on the shoulder. "Hey, tell us what's in the box," she begged.

Uncle Tease just smiled. "You'll find out when we get home."

When they arrived home, Mum and their little brother Alexander were waiting outside to greet Uncle Tease. Dorrie and D.J. carried the big box into the living room.

"I'll help!" Alexander said, jumping up and down.

Dorrie and D.J. started to pull the tape off the top of the box.

"I want to help," Alexander said, as he pushed in beside them to look inside the box.

It was filled with popcorn.

"Goodie!" Alexander shouted. He grabbed a handful of popcorn.

Dorrie and D.J. looked at each other. Popcorn seemed a strange present.

"Where are the real presents?" D.J. asked.

"They're somewhere in the box," Uncle Tease answered.

Coded Messages

"I can feel something," Dorrie said. She pulled her hand out of the box. "Look, it's a torch."

"I've found one, too," D.J. said. "Cool! Mine's green."

"There's another one in there for Alexander," Uncle Tease said. "And there's something else in the box for you older kids."

Dorrie, D.J., and Alexander found a blue torch for Alexander. Down at the bottom of the box, D.J. found a book. It was about Morse code.

"I thought you would have fun flashing messages to each other at night," Uncle Tease said.

D.J. looked up from the code book. "This is great!"

"Thanks, Uncle Tease!" Dorrie said.

Alexander was playing with the button on his torch. Blink, blink.

"Looks like Alexander likes his present, too," Mum said, as she herded the family towards the dining room.

"Katherine thought he would," Uncle Tease said. "She helped me pick them out."

"Who is Katherine?" Mum asked, once dinner was served.

Uncle Tease said, "The wonderful woman I'm going to marry."

As Mum beamed with pleasure, Dorrie slumped back in her chair. Uncle Tease hadn't been teasing during the ride home.

Dorrie didn't say anything during the rest of the dinner. She didn't want Uncle Tease to get married. She could see it now. He wouldn't be fun any more, and he would probably stop spending time with the family.

Uncle Tease said, "Katherine's plane gets in on Saturday morning."

That was the day after tomorrow, Dorrie thought. It didn't give her much time. She had to think of something to make Uncle Tease cancel those wedding plans. Perhaps she could ask D.J. for help.

Dorrie didn't get a chance to talk to D.J. after dinner because Uncle Tease sat down with them to look at the new Morse-code book.

"Before there were telephones, people sent messages by telegraph using Morse code," he explained.

"Was that when you were a kid?" D.J. asked.

Uncle Tease answered, "Thanks a lot! No, you see, the very first message was sent way back in 1844. Morse code is based on dots and dashes, or short and long sounds."

He opened the book and pointed at the page. "You can send torch messages using the code." D.J. and Dorrie each took a code card from the pocket at the back of the book. They practised flashing their names.

Before they knew it, Mum came to say it was time for bed.

"A pillow-fight... a pillow-fight!" Dorrie started to chant. D.J. pulled a pillow from the couch.

Mum grabbed his arm before he had a chance to throw it. "You'll have to postpone your pillow-fight. You have school in the morning."

"We'll have a pillow-fight when Katherine gets here," Uncle Tease promised. "She's a grand-champion pillow-fighter."

Uncle Tease picked up his duffle bag and followed D.J. upstairs to the room they were going to share. "I'll put my things away now, so I won't have to do it in the dark."

That meant Dorrie still wouldn't be able to talk to D.J. She'd have to think of something herself. She picked up her new torch and her code card and went upstairs to her room.

From her bed, she practised writing words on the ceiling. Before long, she fell asleep.

The Presentation

Uncle Tease and D.J. were eating breakfast when Dorrie came down the next morning.

"Isn't today a day off?" Uncle Tease asked. "We should go swimming and then eat ice cream and then…"

"Theodore," Mum said, in her pretend serious voice, "stop teasing them. They'll believe you."

"Oh, Mum, we know he's teasing," D.J. said. "Besides, you know that Uncle Tease promised he'd come to our school with us today."

"I told my teacher that he'd tell our classmates about being in the Peace Corps in Brazil," Dorrie said.

When they got to school, Uncle Tease set up the slide projector in Dorrie's room and Dorrie introduced him.

"This is my Uncle Theodore, but we call him Uncle Tease because he teases us all the time."

Sara Wilcox raised her hand. "My mum says teasing isn't very nice."

Uncle Tease rubbed his chin. "Your mum is right, if teasing is used to hurt someone. As long as you are teasing to make people happy and not to hurt them, then teasing is fine."

He pushed the button and a slide of a monkey showed on the screen. "Hey, has anyone seen my bananas?" Uncle Tease said. Everyone giggled.

"You see, I was just teasing then. I made you laugh, but I didn't hurt anybody except, perhaps, the monkey, who probably wouldn't mind. Now let's have the lights off."

When the room was dark, Uncle Tease told the class about Brazil and the rainforest. Everybody clapped when he finished.

"Any questions?" Uncle Tease asked.

Hands flew up. Uncle Tease pointed to Jeremy.

"With no telephones, how do you keep in touch with people?"

"Good question," Uncle Tease replied. "I used my ham radio."

"But don't ham radios need electricity?" Mrs Jewett asked.

Uncle Tease said, "In remote areas, the radios are battery-powered. My fiancée is an archaeologist. She can work in pretty isolated places.

That's why she encouraged me to get a ham-radio licence."

"You need a licence?" Jeremy asked.

"Yes, and I even had to take a test to get it," Uncle Tease said. "To pass the test, I had to know Morse code."

"Have you ever talked to Dorrie on your radio?" Andy asked.

"No," Uncle Tease said, "but maybe by the next time I travel, Dorrie and D.J. will know enough Morse code to have their licences. Right, Dorrie?"

Dorrie nodded. "It might come in handy some day," she answered.

"Yes, Morse code can help to save lives. Have you heard about when the *Titanic* struck an iceberg?" Uncle Tease asked. "Everyone would have died if a nearby ship hadn't picked up their SOS message. More than 700 people were rescued from the freezing water because of that message."

Uncle Tease could have kept talking all day, but Mrs Jewett came up and stood beside him. "I'm sorry to interrupt, but D.J.'s class is waiting."

"Thanks, guys," Uncle Tease said as he gathered up his things. "I'd better say 'over and out'. That's how hams end all their conversations. It means our time together is over, and I had better go."

Even Sara Wilcox laughed.

The List

The next day, Uncle Tease drove to the airport to pick up Katherine. Alexander went with Dad to get Grandma from the retirement home for her birthday party.

"Don't you want to come with us, Dorrie?" Dad asked.

"We're going to help Mum," Dorrie said. She didn't mention that she needed time to make plans with D.J.

"Would you guys ice Grandma's birthday cake?" Mum asked. "I have to put the roast in the oven."

"Why are you being so strange lately?" D.J. whispered to Dorrie, as they spooned icing onto the cake.

"I'm not being strange," Dorrie said. "I'm just worried. We can't let Uncle Tease marry Katherine. If he gets married, he'll never want to have fun with us any more. He'll start behaving like all the other grown-ups."

"Uncle Tease wouldn't do that." D.J. shook his head.

"Yes he will," Dorrie said.

"OK, what if you're right? How can we stop them getting married? I heard Mum say Katherine's already planned the wedding."

Dorrie licked her fingers and stood back to admire the cake.

"Maybe she'll *un*plan it if we tell her about all of Uncle Tease's girlfriends."

"Well, we can try," D.J. said. "He has had quite a few. Let's make a list."

Dorrie jumped up and got an old envelope from the waste-paper basket. She took a pencil out of the drawer in the coffee table.

"Let's see, there was Suzanne… remember? She was that artist from New York. And what about that woman who wore the black cape? What was her name again?"

"I think the cape woman was Janet," D.J. said.

Dorrie thought. "And there was Emily. Remember Emily? She was pretty cool. She told us about her spider collection."

Mum called from the kitchen, "I can hear a car in the driveway." Dorrie and D.J. went to meet Katherine.

"I know I'm not going to like her," Dorrie whispered.

The Party

When Dorrie and D.J. came into the kitchen, Uncle Tease had just introduced Katherine to Mum.

"Dorrie and D.J., this is my fiancée, Katherine Johnson," Uncle Tease said, putting his arm around Katherine's shoulders. She was tall and slender and, though Dorrie hated to admit it, she looked nice.

D.J. smiled back. "Hi, Katherine."

"I won't bother learning your name," Dorrie said. "Uncle Tease has a new girlfriend every time he comes."

D.J. stifled a giggle. Mum glared at Dorrie, but didn't have a chance to say anything because at that moment Alexander came bouncing in, followed by Dad and Grandma.

Uncle Tease went to greet her, and he took her coat. Dorrie ran to hug her. "Happy Birthday! You smell good, Grandma. Just like roses."

Dorrie couldn't help thinking that it was a good thing she and D.J. weren't going to let Uncle Tease get married. If he were married, he wouldn't have time for Grandma, either. Dorrie looked at Katherine. She was lifting Alexander so he could see the cake.

"Dinner is not quite ready," Mum said. "I need Dad to mash the potatoes. It's his job."

"His job? Hey, mashing the potatoes always used to be my job," Uncle Tease said, winking at Katherine.

"I think we'd better arm-wrestle to see who's going to mash the potatoes for Grandma's party."

"Grandma, you watch him so he doesn't cheat," Dad said.

Grandma smiled. She always loved watching Dad and Uncle Tease. It reminded her of when they were boys.

"Ready, set, go!" D.J. said.

At first Uncle Tease's arm almost touched the table top. Then Uncle Tease flipped Dad's arm over and down onto the table.

"Well, Theodore," Mum said. "You won, so you can start mashing."

"I just let you win," Dad said. "Now I don't have to work."

Mum said, "Yes, you do – you can set the table, and get drinks for everyone. Dorrie and D.J., take Grandma and Katherine into the living room so they can have a chat."

Dorrie decided to sit on the couch next to Katherine. She smiled sweetly. "You remind me of Uncle Tease's last girlfriend, Emily."

"No, you're thinking of Suzanne," D.J. said. "Remember Suzanne? She was the artist. She painted pictures."

"I used to paint," Grandma said.

"You were great, Grandma," D.J. said. He turned to Katherine and said, "Grandma painted that picture over the fireplace. It's where she used to live in the mountains."

Before Dorrie could use the girlfriend list again, Mum said dinner was ready.

"I'll carry Katherine to the table," Uncle Tease said. Katherine giggled when he lifted her high in the air.

During dinner, the twins couldn't use the girlfriend list. The grown-ups talked through the entire meal.

They told Katherine all the old family stories. They even told her about the flash flood that had washed away Grandma's old house where she had lived as a girl.

"You ought to take Katherine up to the mountains to see Grandma's land," Dad said.

"We can do that tomorrow," Uncle Tease said. "We could take some photographs for Grandma. Do you guys want to come?"

"You bet," D.J. said.

After dinner, Katherine helped Mum clean up. Every time Dorrie mentioned one of Uncle Tease's ex-girlfriends, Mum changed the subject. When Dorrie mentioned Veronica, the flight attendant, Mum asked Katherine if she liked flying. When Dorrie mentioned Ann Marie, Mum asked Katherine if she had a middle name.

When Uncle Tease and Katherine took Grandma home, Mum said, "Dorrie, what is wrong with you? You were being so rude to Katherine. I better not hear another word from you about any of Uncle Tease's old girlfriends."

"I won't mention a single one," Dorrie promised and smiled. But she didn't promise that she would stop trying to prevent the wedding.

The Postcard

After dinner, Dorrie and D.J. went into the family room. They had to make up the sofa bed for Katherine.

"Katherine isn't such a bad person, really," Dorrie whispered to D.J. "I just don't want her to marry Uncle Tease."

"She isn't getting the message."

"That's it!" Dorrie exclaimed. "We have to send her a message. You know, like the ones people use when they are trying to stop smoking. We could make a tape to play over and over while she's sleeping."

D.J. shook his head. "I don't think taped messages really work."

D.J. pulled on one end of the couch. Dorrie pulled the other, and the bed popped out.

"You go and get the blankets and I'll put on the pillowcases," Dorrie said.

She picked up one of the pillows Mum had left on the table by Katherine's suitcase. She tucked the pillow under her chin and wiggled on the case. By mistake she knocked a book to the floor. A card fell out from between the pages.

Dorrie picked it up. It was a postcard... a postcard for Katherine.

Dorrie couldn't help noticing it was signed, "With love, Raymond".

Dorrie shook her head. "Oh boy, look at this." She handed the card to D.J.

He read it aloud.

Dear Katherine,

It was great to see you again. You looked terrific. You were very kind to invite me to join you on your exploration of the ruins in Istanbul.

See you soon.

With love,

Raymond

Katherine Johnson

819 Oak Drive

Washington, DC 10010

"Oh, gosh!" exclaimed D.J. "She must just be pretending to love Uncle Tease. She has another boyfriend."

"I know," Dorrie said. "That's one more reason why we have to keep them from getting married. We have to warn Uncle Tease."

Dits and Dahs

The next day, Uncle Tease packed a picnic lunch. Katherine, Dorrie, Uncle Tease, and D.J. climbed into the jeep.

"I hope you packed the torches and code cards," Uncle Tease said. "We can practise Morse code on the way."

On the trip to the mountains, Dorrie asked Katherine where she learnt Morse code.

"We all learnt Morse code from our grandad. He told us to forget how the code looked, and to think about how it sounded," Katherine answered.

"What do you mean?" D.J. asked.

"Remember how *Twinkle*, *Twinkle*, *Little Star* sounds?" Katherine said.

D.J. and Dorrie both sang the first line. "When you first learnt that song, you learnt to hear the sounds, and not the actual notes. You do the same thing with Morse code."

"Tell them about the dits and dahs," Uncle Tease encouraged.

"Most hams," Katherine said, "think of dits and dahs instead of dots and dashes. A dah is three times longer than a dit. When a dit is in a string, it is shortened to just di. So an 'A' is a di-dah. An 'E' is just a dit."

"There are some really cool combinations to learn," Uncle Tease said. "For example, the letter 'V' is an easy code to remember. Think 'V is for victory'. Then say the code di-di-di-dah, or 'this-is-a-V'."

"Hey! It's just like the first four notes of Beethoven's *Fifth Symphony*," Dorrie said.

"The 'M' is my favourite," Uncle Tease said. "Say dah-dah. It has the same rhythm as saying 'Ta-da'!"

Dorrie and D.J. practised the rest of the way to the mountains. Uncle Tease patted Katherine's shoulder. "Hold on. We're just about there. It can get pretty bumpy as we get near the creek."

"It can't be any worse than some of the roads around Istanbul," she said.

Dorrie and D.J. exchanged glances. They were thinking the same thing. Istanbul was where Katherine was going to see Raymond.

The True Story

The jeep came to a bumpy stop in a large clearing. "It's so beautiful up here!" Katherine said.

"I think we should have our picnic here, close to the car," Uncle Tease said. "Then we won't have to carry everything across the creek."

"Maybe we should take the photos first, before we eat," Dorrie said. "It looks like it's going to rain and it's getting gloomy. We don't want to wait until it's too dark and cloudy to get any good photos."

Uncle Tease looked at the dark sky. "You know, Dorrie, you might be right about that rain. What about taking Katherine over to show her where Grandma's house used to be? I'll get the food ready."

"Good idea," Katherine said. "Lead the way, kids."

"We usually cross over by Rock City," D.J. said.

The twins pointed to a place where giant boulders seemed to fill the creek. "There's Rock City," D.J. said. "The rocks are so close together it's easy to cross, unless the creek is really high."

D.J. scampered over the rocks.

"I'm not sure I can get across – what if I fall in?" Katherine said.

Dorrie led Katherine over to the rocks. "Just follow me. I'll show you an easy way. It's all in knowing where to go," Dorrie said.

"I'll race you to the field," D.J. called. He sprinted off. Dorrie pointed to the grass. "If you'd been here a month ago, you'd have seen wild flowers everywhere."

"Speaking of flowers," Katherine said. "I thought you could be a flower girl at our wedding. But you're much more grown up than I'd expected. Would you rather light the candles?"

Dorrie couldn't think of what to say. Luckily, D.J. came running back towards them. "You brought the camera, didn't you?" he asked Dorrie.

"Uh, no," Dorrie said. "I thought you had it."

D.J. glared at her and shook his head. "It must be on the seat in the jeep. We'll have to go back and get it."

He turned to Katherine and said, "Will you wait here? We'll be back in a few minutes."

Before Katherine could say a word, Dorrie and D.J. ran back across the pathway of boulders.

Uncle Tease was surprised to see Dorrie and D.J. when they came running up. It had started to rain.

"Where's Katherine? Has anything happened?" He sounded worried.

"Nothing's wrong," D.J. said. "We just wanted a chance to talk to you for a few minutes without Katherine. We think something bad will happen if you get married."

"You two have been trying to get me to break off my engagement, haven't you?" Uncle Tease asked.

Dorrie and D.J. nodded.

"Why?" Uncle Tease asked.

"Because if you get married, we won't see you so often," Dorrie said.

"You won't want to do things with us any more."

"Let me see if I've got this right," he said. "You think I'll stop loving you just because I'm getting married?"

"We just thought you wouldn't love us as much," Dorrie said.

Uncle Tease laughed. "I can understand that you might feel like that. But you know that I can't be here with you all the time. Sometimes I get tired of being alone."

Dorrie started to feel ashamed of herself when she heard that. Then she remembered her other concern.

"But what about that Raymond guy?" she blurted out.

"Raymond?" Uncle Tease asked.

"Yeah," D.J. said. "That man who is going to Istanbul."

Uncle Tease really started to laugh. "Do you mean Professor Raymond?

He's seventy-five years old and married. He's one of Katherine's old professors from university."

"So you've known about him all along?" Dorrie asked quietly.

"Of course," Uncle Tease said. "Now, will you give Katherine a chance?"

"I will," D.J. said.

"Me, too," Dorrie agreed.

Uncle Tease rumpled D.J.'s hair and gave Dorrie a big hug.

"I'm going to get Katherine," Dorrie said, "and tell her I'm sorry we've been so mean."

She raced off towards the creek, through the rain that was now falling in huge, pounding drops.

The Flash Flood

By the time Dorrie reached the creek, the rain was coming down in torrents. To make things even worse, all of the rain that had fallen further up in the mountains was now rushing down into the swollen creek. The creek was nearly a metre higher than it had been only twenty minutes earlier.

Dorrie was afraid that Katherine might try to cross at Rock City. The rocks would be too slippery now. The current was too fast. Dorrie had to warn her.

"Katherine!" she called. But Dorrie's voice didn't carry over the crashing thunder and pounding rain.

Dorrie knew better than to cross the slippery rocks in the swollen stream, but Katherine – who wasn't used to mountain flash floods – might try.

Then Dorrie remembered the bridge further downstream, and she knew what she had to do. She pulled her torch out of her backpack. Its bright beam would shine through the rain.

Dorrie flashed a "D" and an "O". She remembered those letters from her name. She shielded the code card from the rain so she could look up "W", "N", "S", and "T". She remembered the "R" and the "E". "A" was easy – di-dah. So was "M" – dah-dah.

"DOWNSTREAM".

Dorrie kept repeating the code, over and over, as she walked downstream.

She was moving slowly, hoping that Katherine would understand.

Dorrie was almost to the bridge when the rain stopped as suddenly as it had started. It had been just another mountain cloudburst. "Katherine!" Dorrie called.

This time Katherine heard her. Dorrie ran across the bridge and she threw her arms around Katherine. Katherine hugged her back.

Dorrie said, "I was so afraid that you'd try to get across the wet rocks."

"I almost did," Katherine said, "but I knew you must have been flashing 'downstream' for a reason."

D.J. and Uncle Tease, both dripping wet, came charging through the wet trees. "You're safe! You're both safe!"

"We certainly are," Katherine said. "My heroes, Dorrie and Samuel Morse, saved the day."

Once they were all back at home, D.J. told Mum and Dad about their failed plans to keep Katherine from marrying Uncle Tease.

"Nothing worked," Dorrie said.

Dad laughed when Uncle Tease told them about Raymond's postcard, but Mum looked really angry. "You didn't really read Katherine's mail, did you?"

Dorrie nodded sheepishly.

"I understand. It's very hard not to read a postcard," Katherine said. "Before my older brother got married, I tried to trick his fiancée into cancelling the wedding. I knew she had hay fever, so I put a big bouquet of flowers on the table when she came to dinner. I hoped she'd decide she was allergic to us, but she didn't."

Dorrie and D.J. laughed.

"Actually," Katherine continued, "I found out it is really fun having a sister-in-law."

"I'm sure the twins will like having you for an aunt," Mum said.

"Gosh," D.J. said, "what do you want us to call you after you and Uncle Tease get married?"

"Why don't you kids decide on a name," Katherine said.

D.J. thought for a moment. "How about Aunt K?"

"Or Aunt Katie?" Mum suggested.

"I have a better idea," Dorrie said. She whispered something to D.J.

He nodded. "Perfect, Dorrie."

"Well," Dorrie said, "Uncle Tease has a special name. We thought you should, too. We decided to call you Auntie Awesome."

And when Dorrie said that, she felt pretty awesome, too.

The International Morse Code

Alphabet:

A	B	C	D
• —	— • • •	— • — •	— • •
di-dah	dah-di-di-dit	dah-di-dah-dit	dah-di-dit

E	F	G	H
•	• • — •	— — •	• • • •
dit	di-di-dah-dit	dah-dah-dit	di-di-di-dit

I	J	K	L
• •	• — — —	— • —	• — • •
di-dit	di-dah-dah-dah	dah-di-dah	di-dah-di-dit

M	N	O	P
— —	— •	— — —	• — — •
dah-dah	dah-dit	dah-dah-dah	di-dah-dah-dit

Q	R	S	T
— — • —	• — •	• • •	—
dah-dah-di-dah	di-dah-dit	di-di-dit	dah

U	V	W	X
• • —	• • • —	• — —	— • • —
di-di-dah	di-di-di-dah	di-dah-dah	dah-di-di-dah

Y	Z
— • — —	— — • •
dah-di-dah-dah	dah-dah-di-dit

Numerals:

1	2	3	4	5
• — — — —	• • — — —	• • • — —	• • • • —	• • • • •
di-dah-dah-dah-dah	di-di-dah-dah-dah	di-di-di-dah-dah	di-di-di-di-dah	di-di-di-di-dit

6	7	8	9	0
— • • • •	— — • • •	— — — • •	— — — — •	— — — — —
dah-di-di-di-dit	dah-dah-di-di-dit	dah-dah-dah-di-dit	dah-dah-dah-dah-dit	dah-dah-dah-dah-dah

From the Author

I live in the sweetheart city of Loveland, Colorado, with my husband, who creates waterfowl sculpture. We have five grown-up children, who are all embarking on exciting careers. When I am not working in the classroom, I am usually writing, playing tennis, or teaching toddlers to swim.

I wrote *Uncle Tease* because of all the kind and gentle teasing that has brought laughter to my life.

Ellen Javernick

From the Illustrator

I live in Minneapolis, Minnesota, where I paint, draw, and work on computer and video art. When I illustrate a children's book, I listen to the voices of the author and editor, then make a "quiet space" inside myself to let these voices speak. After a while, I begin to create the images, which sometimes come easily and, at other times, come in fits and starts. But, it's all worthwhile when I see the results in a beautiful book.

Liz Dodson

FRIENDS AND FRIENDSHIP
Uncle Tease
PS I Love You, Gramps
Friendship in Action
Midnight Rescue
Nightmare
You Can Canoe!

ACTION AND ADVENTURE
Dinosaur Girl
Amelia Earhart
Taking to the Air
No Trouble at All!
River Runners
The Midnight Pig

WILD AND WONDERFUL
Winter Survival
Peter the Pumpkin-Eater
Because of Walter
Humphrey
Hairy Little Critters
The Story of Small Fry

ALL THE WORLD'S A STAGE
All the World's a Stage!
Which Way, Jack?
The Bad Luck of King Fred
Famous Animals
Puppets
The Wish Fish

Written by **Ellen Javernick**
Illustrated by **Liz Dodson**
Edited by **Rebecca McEwen**
Designed by **Gary Haney**

© 1997 Shortland Publications Inc.
All rights reserved.

09 08 07
12 11 10 9 8 7

Published in Australia and New Zealand by MIMOSA/McGraw-Hill,
8 Yarra Street, Hawthorn, Victoria 3122, Australia
Published in the United Kingdom by Kingscourt/McGraw-Hill,
Shoppenhangers Road, Maidenhead, Berkshire SL6 2QL

Printed in China through Colorcraft Ltd., Hong Kong
ISBN: 1-57257-735-5